HORSING AROUND

Cross-Country and Endurance

Summit Free Public Library

Penny Dowdy

Crabtree Publishing Company

www.crabtreebooks.com

Crabtree Publishing Company
www.crabtreebooks.com

Author: Penny Dowdy
Editor: Lynn Peppas
Proofreader: Crystal Sikkens
Editorial director: Kathy Middleton
Production coordinator: Katherine Berti
Prepress technician: Katherine Berti
Coordinating editor: Chester Fisher
Series editor: Sue Labella
Project manager: Kumar Kunal (Q2AMEDIA)
Art direction: Dibakar Acharjee (Q2AMEDIA)
Cover design: Shruti Aggarwal (Q2AMEDIA)
Design: Shruti Aggarwal (Q2AMEDIA)
Photo research: Ekta Sharma (Q2AMEDIA)
Reading consultant: Cecilia Minden, Ph.D.

Cover: A rider competes in a cross-country competition.

Title page: Two riders compete in the Al Reef Endurance Horse Race in Abu Dhabi, UAE.

Photographs:
Cover: Mikhail Kondrashov/Istockphoto (main image), Emberiza/Shutterstock, Tischenko Irina/Shutterstock, P1: Adam Cukrowski/Photolibrary (main image), Emberiza/Shutterstock, P4: Chris Skelton/Getty Images, P5: Margo Harrison/ BigStockPhoto, Lukiyanova Natalia/Frenta/Shutterstock, P6: Junji Kurokawa/Associated Press, P7: Adam Cukrowski/Photolibrary, Lukiyanova Natalia/Frenta/Shutterstock, P8: Harris & Ewing/ Library Of Congress, P9: Str/Associated Press, Lukiyanova Natalia/Frenta/Shutterstock, P10: Bob Langrish, P11 : Bob Langrish, Lukiyanova Natalia/Frenta/Shutterstock, P12: Rob Carr/Associated Press, P13: Tim Graham/Getty Images, Lukiyanova Natalia/Frenta/Shutterstock, P14: James Boardman/Rex Features, Lukiyanova Natalia/Frenta/Shutterstock, P15: James Boardman/Rex Features, P16: Caren Firouz/Reuters, P17: Nir Elias/Reuters, Lukiyanova Natalia/Frenta/Shutterstock, P18: Danita Delimont/Alamy, P19: Ali Jarekji/Reuters, Lukiyanova Natalia/Frenta/Shutterstock, P20: Margo Harrison/ Shutterstock, P21: Rick Hyman/Istockphoto, Lukiyanova Natalia/Frenta/Shutterstock, P22: SCFotos/Alamy, P23: Craig Lister/Istockphoto, Lukiyanova Natalia/ Frenta/ Shutterstock, P24: Manfred Grebler/Photolibrary, P25(t): Christopher Lee/ Getty Images, P25(b): Tim Graham/Alamy, Lukiyanova Natalia/Frenta/Shutterstock, P26: Juniors Bildarchiv/ Photolibrary, P27: Alen MacWeeney/Corbis, Lukiyanova Natalia/Frenta/Shutterstock, P28: Phil Walter/Getty Images, P29: Susan Walsh/Associated Press, Lukiyanova Natalia/ Frenta/Shutterstock, P31: James Boardman/Rex Features, Folio Image: Wendy Kaveney Photography/Shutterstock

Library and Archives Canada Cataloguing in Publication

Dowdy, Penny
Cross-country and endurance / Penny Dowdy.

(Horsing around)
Includes index.
ISBN 978-0-7787-4980-6 (bound).--ISBN 978-0-7787-4996-7 (pbk.)

1. Cross-country (Horsemanship)--Juvenile literature. 2. Endurance riding (Horsemanship)--Juvenile literature. I. Title. II. Series: Horsing around (St. Catharines, Ont.)

SF295.6.D69 2009   j798.2'4   C2009-903882-X

Library of Congress Cataloging-in-Publication Data

Dowdy, Penny.
Cross-country and endurance / Penny Dowdy.
p. cm. -- (Horsing around)
Includes index.
ISBN 978-0-7787-4996-7 (pbk. : alk. paper) -- ISBN 978-0-7787-4980-6 (reinforced library binding : alk. paper)
1. Cross-country (Horsemanship)--Juvenile literature. 2. Endurance riding (Horsemanship)--Juvenile literature. I. Title. II. Series.

SF295.6.D68 2010
798.2'4--dc22

2009024756

Crabtree Publishing Company
www.crabtreebooks.com   1-800-387-7650

Published in Canada
Crabtree Publishing
616 Welland Ave.
St. Catharines, ON
L2M 5V6

Published in the United States
Crabtree Publishing
PMB16A
350 Fifth Ave., Suite 3308
New York, NY 10118

Published in the United Kingdom
Crabtree Publishing
Maritime House
Basin Road North, Hove
BN41 1WR

Published in Australia
Crabtree Publishing
386 Mt. Alexander Rd.
Ascot Vale (Melbourne)
VIC 3032

Contents

Cross-Country 101

Cross-country events take place on an **obstacle course**. An obstacle course is a trail or track. The obstacles are objects blocking the horse and rider's path. The horse must jump the obstacles to finish the race.

The typical cross-country **course** is a few miles (kilometers) long. It has dozens of jumps or obstacles. The horse and rider must finish the course in about 11 minutes. If they do not, they receive points against them. They also receive points if they do not complete all the jumps. The cross-country race combines speed, **endurance**, and jumping skills. It can also present risks to the horse and rider.

Great jumping skills are needed on a cross-country course.

The rider watches the horse's energy and breathing while they complete the cross-country course.

Cross-country can be a single competition. However, in contests such as the Olympics, it is part of a group called **eventing**. The eventing contest includes dressage, how jumping, and cross-country. A rider who participates in eventing should keep a close check on his or her horse. A horse that is pushed too hard in one part of the contest could wear down quickly. It could become too tired for the remaining parts. Eventing is a test of how well a rider knows a horse's body and spirit.

5

Endurance 101

A horse works much harder in an endurance competition than in cross-country. Horses and riders go about 12 miles (19 km) or more over a set period of time. In some endurance events, horses go 100 miles (161 km) or more. The horses must be in excellent condition.

Endurance rides go through natural trails. A good course has hills, water, and changes in the **terrain**. The trail should be in its natural condition. The obstacles horses jump are natural, too. The trail must be marked with special flags and course markers. You can imagine how easy it would be to get off the trail when riding in such a long race! Riders must watch their course during the ride to stay on track.

Horses and riders take on hilly terrain.

Two things must happen in order to win an endurance race. First, the horse has to finish the course. Second, a horse must have a normal heart rate (after a rest) at the end of the race.

This checks that riders have not pushed their horses too hard. The winner is the horse that finishes first and has a healthy heart rate. Many endurance races have a second award. A vet checks the fitness of every horse. The horse that is most fit wins the Best Condition award. This encourages riders to keep their horses in great physical condition.

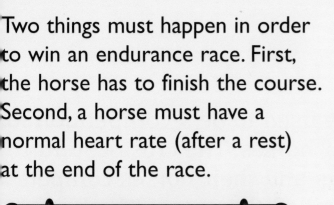

FACT BOX

Many North American endurance rides are 100 miles (161 km) long. It can take two days time to complete the course. A rider must be able to camp out with a horse and ride long distances.

Some endurance courses are through hot deserts.

History

The cross-country ride used to be a competition for military men and their horses. The cross-country competition let soldiers and their horses compete to show how fit and skilled they were. The horses had to be able to handle long distances, uneven ground, and heavy loads.

Horses were the only mode of transportation until the automobile was invented. Horses were as important to war as weapons. They moved troops and carried equipment. They served in battle no matter where it was. The horses had to be able to handle all kinds of terrain, and jump over obstacles. The cross-country race started in the 1800s as a soldiers' race between Berlin and Vienna, over 300 miles (482 km). Then France held its own race, called the *Raid Militaire*. In 1912, officials made cross-country an Olympic event.

Cross-country started as part of a contest for soldiers and their horses.

FACT BOX

A horse could wear down while traveling to a battle site. That could be trouble for a soldier if the horse was tired when it came time to fight. Soldiers made sure their horses had water and rested. The horses needed their energy for battle.

Obstacles, such as this fence, were dangerous to both horse and rider.

The original cross-country race was long and grueling. The trails were long, like today's endurance races, but had higher jumps and more difficult obstacles. Many horses fell or tripped in these races. In the 1968 Olympics alone, two horses died from exhaustion on the course. People concerned with the health of the animals complained.

Since then, cross-country and endurance became two separate sports. Cross-country uses a shorter course and is part of the three-day eventing. Endurance became a single sport where horses and riders cover long distances. Creating two sports where there used to be one has greatly reduced the number of injuries to horses.

Care and Handling

In cross-country or endurance, a rider must always keep a check on their horse. A horse can pull muscles when it gallops long distances. It can get leg injuries and foot problems from jumping. A rider must always be aware of the horse's health.

A veterinarian (vet) is an animal doctor. The vet checks each horse before it starts a race. This takes about ten minutes. The vet checks the horse's temperature, breathing, and pulse. All of these tell whether the horse is in condition to run a hard race. The vet also looks at the horse's feet and muscles. Finally, the vet looks for signs of sores on the skin from saddles or other **tack**. If any part of the vet's check is a cause for concern, the horse may not be allowed to compete.

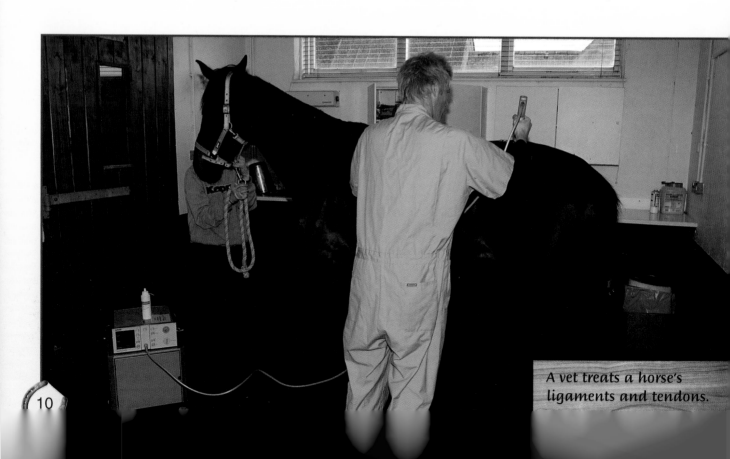

A vet treats a horse's ligaments and tendons.

A rider guides a Belgian Warmblood over an obstacle at an Olympic event.

The way a rider handles a horse can affect the horse's health. A rider should guide a horse straight toward a jump. Jumping an obstacle at an angle can cause the horse's hind legs to trip. The rider should also judge the kinds of obstacles the horse is about to take. If the horse approaches a water obstacle, the rider will slow the horse down. This helps keep the horse from slipping on muddy ground. If the ground is steep, the rider will guide the horse slowly so it does not stumble.

5 Training

A horse must know both running and jumping to compete in cross-country. Horses that become bored or tired during training do not learn well. The rider must also make training interesting and fun!

Training a horse for endurance takes time. A rider starts with short rides, and slowly increases the length of a workout. In time, the horse and rider may work together for an hour a day. Riders do not take their horses on long-distance rides too often. Instead, the rider takes the horse on a long distance ride every few weeks. The rider checks the time for each ride. As the ride becomes easier for the horse, the rider can increase the speed or distance.

Riders depend on coaches to help them train for races.

The rider teaches the horse signals so that the horse can prepare for a jump.

A horse must learn to jump all obstacles in a cross-country course. The horse starts by stepping over small things, such as a piece of wood. Gradually, the rider or coach increases the size of the obstacle.

Slowly, the horse becomes comfortable with each small increase. The rider shows the horse the kinds of obstacles it will be jumping. This makes the horse feel comfortable around the obstacles. During training, the rider also teaches the horse different signals. The horse learns the signals for walk, run, and leap. Finally, the horse learns to trust the rider enough to jump when he or she gives the signal.

6

Equipment

A cross-country rider and horse have special equipment. Much of it protects the rider from injury. Some equipment helps the rider control the horse. The rules for each event describe exactly what equipment is or is not allowed.

Cross-country riders fall. It is not a matter of if, but when. A helmet protects the head. A safety vest covers the chest and back. This protects a rider who falls or hits a branch. It also gives the rider extra padding on his or her spine. Finally, the rider wears an armband with medical information on it. This helps if the rider is knocked out. Emergency workers will have information they need to care for the rider.

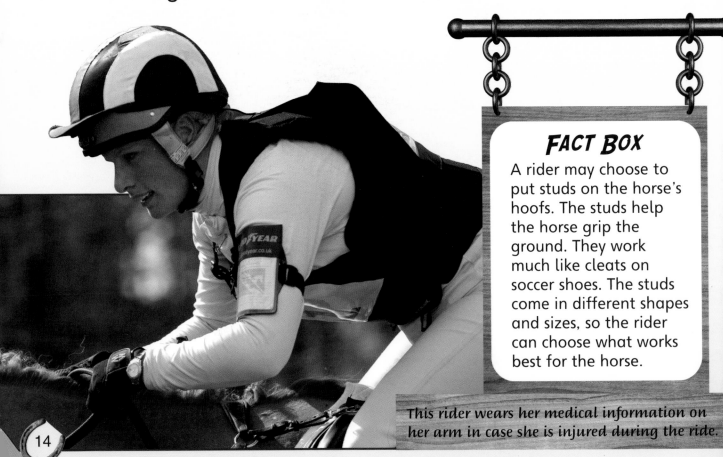

FACT BOX

A rider may choose to put studs on the horse's hoofs. The studs help the horse grip the ground. They work much like cleats on soccer shoes. The studs come in different shapes and sizes, so the rider can choose what works best for the horse.

This rider wears her medical information on her arm in case she is injured during the ride.

medical armband

safety vest

saddle

helmet

bridle

reins

bit

spurs

The labels name the parts of the horse and rider's equipment.

The rider also has equipment to control the horse. A whip corrects the horse. The whip can also be a signal for a **reluctant** horse to move. Spurs do the same thing. Riders do not use spurs or whips to hurt the horse. They use the tools just enough to get the horse's attention. The horse has equipment, too. A cross-country saddle is cushioned so the rider feels comfortable on a rough course. These special saddles can cost up to $2,000! The bridle fits over the horse's head to keep headgear in place. The reins and metal bit attach to the bridle. The bit sits in the horse's mouth. A rider tugs the reins. This moves the bit and signals in what direction the horse should go.

Cross-Country Events

Cross-country riders can compete in many races in addition to the Olympics. Riders can race in large world-wide events or small, local races. Riders of all ages and abilities can enjoy the sport.

Concours Complet International (CCI) is a three-day cross-country event. Riders from any country can compete. Many believe the CCI is harder than the Olympics. Each horse and rider must jump over 45 obstacles. The CCI offers easier courses for less experienced riders and younger horses. It is one of the most important cross-country events in the world.

The Concours International Combiné (CIC) is like the CCI, but is only one day long. The Pan Am Games and World Championships also give riders a chance to compete with riders from other countries.

This rider competed in the 2008 Beijing Olympics.

This international event takes place in the United Arab Emirates.

FACT BOX

Some cross-country contests are held indoors. This allows riders and horses to ride in any weather. Britain's most important national cross-country event is held indoors. This means all of the grounds and obstacles must be man-made.

Many countries hold contests to find the nations' best cross-country riders. Many good riders and horses use these national events to earn invitations to the international contests.

Often cross-country riders start by competing in local races. Clubs for horse owners invite riders to compete in their small events. Educational groups such as 4-H also hold races for the young members to try. No matter what your age or skill level, there is a cross-country race for you!

8 Endurance Events

There are fewer endurance events for **equestrians** than cross-country events. Why is this? Endurance is not part of the Olympics. Perhaps there is less need for smaller events to rate endurance riders.

Still, there are some big endurance competitions. The World Equestrian Games happens every four years. The games give endurance riders the chance to compete on a world-class level. The endurance course in the World Equestrian Games is 100 miles (160 km) long. Countries and continents may hold large endurance events, too. The European Endurance Championship gives the best riders from Europe a chance to compete. The course is the same length as the World Equestrian Games.

Some endurance competitions are casual. In this ride, there is no winner.

The American Endurance Ride Conference holds a championship ride every year. Riders can compete in a 50-mile (80-km) or 100-mile (160-km) ride throughout North America.

Riders also can compete in many small events. The Endurance Riders Association of British Columbia holds six events a year. In the United States, many clubs and private groups such as the Mountain Region Endurance Riders, also hold rides. Riders can see some of the most beautiful parts of the country while they practice their sport.

FACT BOX

Taking part in endurance rides without judges is a good way to practice for the real thing. Riders and coaches can practice techniques without worrying about points. Some endurance events are not timed at all. They are just rides without competition between riders.

This endurance race took place near the mountains in Jordan.

Obstacles

A cross-country rider can see 12 or more different obstacles in one race. Some obstacles sit alone on the course. Several can also be placed together. Many obstacles are built for cross-country races. They are decorated to look like nature. In endurance, the obstacles are part of nature.

Most obstacles are fences or walls. These jumps can be quite tricky. A bullfinch is a wall with tall bushes growing out of it. The bushes grow so high that the horse cannot jump over them. Instead, the horse must jump through them! A trakehner has a fence above ground with a ditch beneath it.

This type of fence can spook a horse. The horse might think it will land in the ditch, rather than past it. Time and experience eventually help the horse understand that it will be landing on the ground.

This rider takes the horse into a water obstacle.

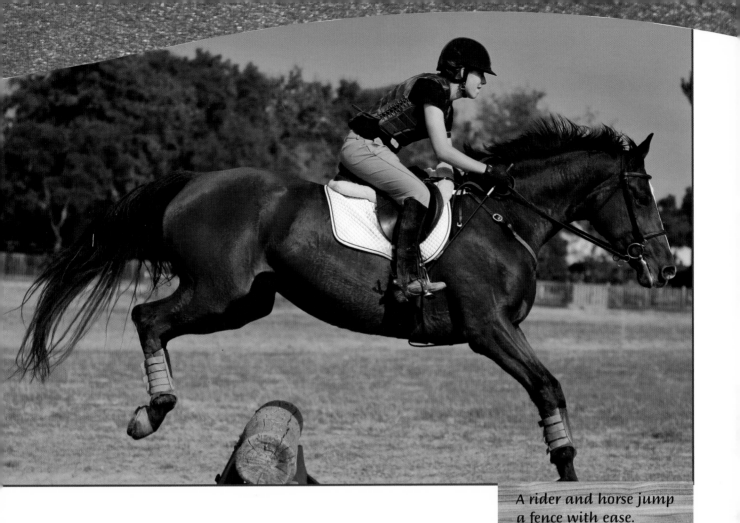

A rider and horse jump a fence with ease.

Many obstacles have lower land on one side. The horse jumps and comes down on ground that is lower than where it started. The horse cannot see this lower ground ahead of time. The horse must have great trust in the rider to take these jumps.

Water obstacles give horses different problems. When you are in water, the water slows your movements. The same is true for horses. If the horse runs up to the water quickly, the change in speed can throw the horse off-balance. Sometimes horses must jump on or over islands in the water. Climbing out of water obstacles can be difficult, too.

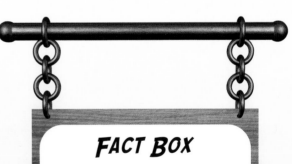

FACT BOX

Most jumping equestrian sports have obstacles that move if the horse hits them. In cross-country, however, the obstacles are solid. They do not move when they are hit. If a horse misses this kind of jump, there can be more injury to the horse and rider.

Rules and Judging

Equestrian organizations may have their own rules for competitions. Judges must know the rules for each contest in order to score the event correctly. Many rules come from the Fédération Equestre Internationale (FEI). The Olympics and most major competitions use the FEI's rules.

Each rider starts with a score of zero. Judges add points as riders or horses make mistakes. Mistakes can happen while jumping. Horses and riders also receive points for not finishing quickly enough. There are three kinds of faults. The first is disobedience. Disobedience is when a horse does not follow a command. For example, the rider signals the horse to jump. The horse stops before the obstacle or turns away from it. This disobedience costs 20 points or more.

The rider follows FEI rules on each ride to earn as few points as possible.

This horse commits a disobedience, causing the rider to fall.

The second type of fault is a fall. If the rider falls, the rider and horse are out of the race. The third type of fault is a willful delay. A rider may slow the horse at the end of the race. This will bring the horse's heart rate down. Then the horse appears to be in better shape than it is. A willful delay costs 20 points.

The races have many judges. They work in all parts of the course. Each obstacle has someone nearby. Timekeepers stand at the beginning and end of the course. Other judges are there to inspect the horses and answer questions.

FACT BOX

FEI rules are very strict. A horse and a rider who fail to finish a course, can be kept out of the next race. Any horse that falls on a cross-country course must retire. This means the horse can never compete in cross-country again.

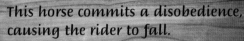

23

11 Risks

Many riders enjoy competing in cross-country and endurance. The sport gives riders a chance to spend time with animals they love. But the sport is also one of the most dangerous sports in the world.

Many riders and horses are injured every year. Most of the injuries come from falls. Horses can break a bone simply by running. High speeds and the weight of a rider put stress on leg bones. Other falls happen at obstacles. The obstacles are solid. If a horse hits one, both the horse and rider are likely to fall. Broken bones are often **fatal** for a horse. People can die from these accidents as well. Riders may be kicked or crushed by a horse.

Running at this high speed can cause a horse to break a leg.

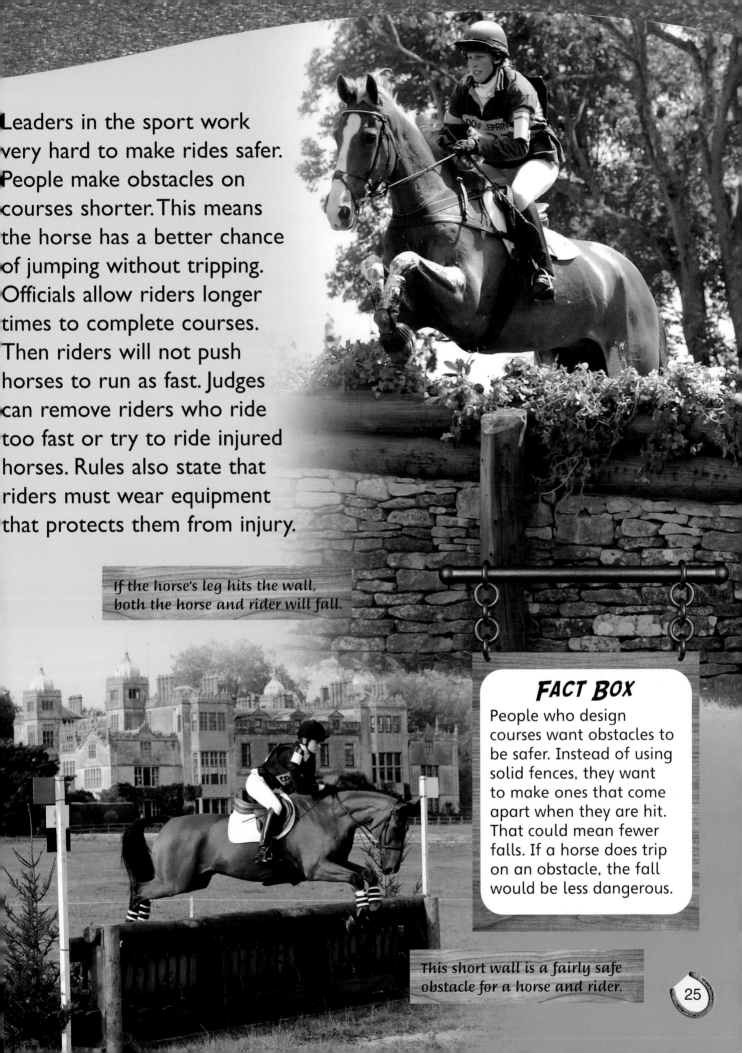

Leaders in the sport work very hard to make rides safer. People make obstacles on courses shorter. This means the horse has a better chance of jumping without tripping. Officials allow riders longer times to complete courses. Then riders will not push horses to run as fast. Judges can remove riders who ride too fast or try to ride injured horses. Rules also state that riders must wear equipment that protects them from injury.

If the horse's leg hits the wall, both the horse and rider will fall.

FACT BOX

People who design courses want obstacles to be safer. Instead of using solid fences, they want to make ones that come apart when they are hit. That could mean fewer falls. If a horse does trip on an obstacle, the fall would be less dangerous.

This short wall is a fairly safe obstacle for a horse and rider.

Best Breeds

All breeds of horses can compete and perform well in cross-country. The rules allow any horse breeds to complete the course. Even donkeys have been known to compete in cross-country and endurance races! Read on to learn what horses make a good choice for cross-country or endurance.

Some riders like using draft horses for cross-country. To look at a draft horse, you might be surprised. This horse is large and well built. It does not seem like it would be a good jumping horse. However, a draft horse's legs are sturdy. It can land jumps and stay steady where other horses might fall.

This beautiful draft horse uses its strong legs to compete in cross-country.

A horse with strength and stamina is what's needed for cross-country and endurance.

Irish sport horses are smaller than draft horses. They also do very well in cross-country and endurance. These horses have very strong back legs. This makes them terrific jumpers. They have both strength and **stamina**. Irish sport horses have all the qualities a rider wants.

Thoroughbreds are great runners. Equestrian fans see them most on race tracks. A Thoroughbred that can jump makes a good cross-country horse, though. A mixed breed that is a cross between an Irish sport horse and a Thoroughbred makes an ideal horse for cross-country and endurance.

FACT BOX

Some riders like riding gaited horses for cross-country. A gaited horse is a breed that does not trot. They never have a three-beat movement. At a medium speed, a gaited horse has a four-beat movement. The ride has more balance. The rider does not bounce as much.

13 Superstars

When cross-country became an Olympic sport in 1912, riders became stars. Cross-country riders can have long careers. The best riders can collect a large number of medals. Great riders can use many horses in their careers. Some of those horses have become famous, too.

The FEI calls Mark Todd of New Zealand the Rider of the 20th Century. In Todd's first World Championship, his horse failed to finish the course. Todd loved the competitive sport, so he moved to England to train. He became the best eventing rider in history. Todd has competed in six Olympic Games. He won the Olympic gold two times and bronze once. Todd also won the World Championships twice and the European Championship once. Todd retired in 2000 after the Olympics. In 2009, at the age of 53, he came back to ride full-time.

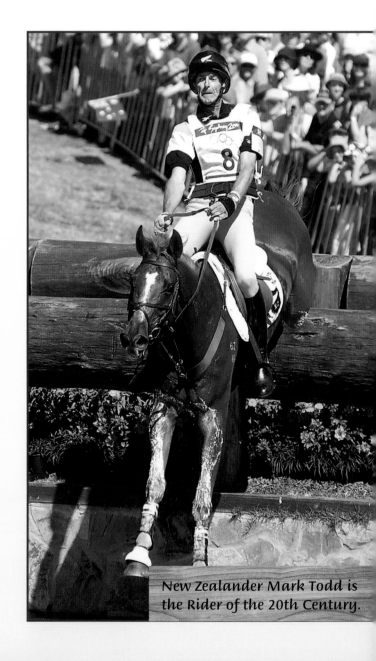

New Zealander Mark Todd is the Rider of the 20th Century.

Amy Tryon rides Poggio II
in the 2008 Beijing Olympics.

FACT BOX

Badminton is one of Great Britain's best-known cross-country events. In 1994, Mark Todd entered the event. He broke off a stirrup in the beginning of the race. He rode and jumped most of the course this way. Todd won the race with only one foot connected to the saddle!

Any breed of horse can compete in cross-country, which means a horse from any background may turn out to be a great athlete. American Amy Tryon bought a horse she named Poggio II. He had been a racehorse, but was not a winner. Then he became a pack horse. Within four years, Poggio II and Tryon rode in the World Championships. In 2002, the pair helped the U.S. team win gold at the World Equestrian Games.

Facts and Figures

Since Olympic athletes do not get paid for winning, many riders need to find ways to make a living while they train for their sport. In the 2008 Olympics, medal winning riders held jobs such as soldiers, builders, dentists, farmers, and managers for other athletes. Many riders work as coaches for young or new riders. One British bronze-medalist, William Pitt-Fox, is riding coach to the singer Madonna!

If a horse club holds many cross-country events, then chances are the club has a course already in place. However, when a city wins a bid for the Olympics or the FEI World Cup, the planners of the event want to make a great impression. This means that new courses must be designed. In the Beijing Olympics, a golf course in Hong Kong was used for the course. All of the obstacles had to be built for the event, including a fence designed to look like the Great Wall of China, a wooden fish in the middle of a water obstacle, a giant set of chopsticks, and fences carved as wooden dragons. After the event, major repairs were needed to the golf course to return it to playable condition.

Cross-country courses used to be extremely difficult for horses and riders. In the 1932 Olympic Games in Los Angeles, only two horses completed the cross-country event. The rest did not finish the ride due to injuries. This means that the gold and silver medals were awarded, but the bronze medal was not. The 1936 Olympics had a somewhat safer course, but just over half of the 50 horses were able to finish. In 1956, the Olympic course in Melbourne, Australia was so muddy that 68 horses fell on the course. The FEI World Equestrian Games has an Endurance competition as one of its events. The 99-mile (159-km) course is a challenge not just in the obstacles, but in the sheer length of the course.

In the 2006 Games, the fastest rider, Miguel Vila Ubach of Spain, completed the course in 9.2 hours. That's a very long ride! The 2006 Games had 159 riders start the course, but only 65 finished. The remaining 94 horses became injured on the course, were retired due to a fall, or were eliminated for breaking FEI rules! Not finishing is fairly common for endurance competitions. The most famous competition in the United States is the Western States Trail Ride, also known as the Tevis Cup. Generally only about half the horses and riders finish the course. The ride is 100 miles (161 km) long, starting at 5:15 in the morning near Truckee, California. Riders take a trail through the Sierra Nevada Mountains and Squaw Valley. The ride must be completed by 5:15 the following morning. Since many riders are on horseback at night, the ride is always scheduled during a full moon. Unfortunately, the 2008 competition was cancelled due to the wildfires burning near the trail.

Glossary

course Path or trail

endurance The ability to last in a strenuous activity, such as a long-distance equestrian event

equestrian Related to horses

eventing Equestrian sport made up of show jumping, dressage, and cross-country

fatal Deadly

obstacle course A path with blockages that the racer must jump

reluctant Hesitant

stamina The ability to last in a strenuous activity

tack Equipment such as reins, saddle, stirrups, bits, and bridles

terrain Type of ground or land

Index

Printed in the U.S.A.—CC